book is to be returned on or before

THIS WALKER BOOK BELONGS TO:

_____

_____

_____

_____

First published 1992 by
Walker Books Ltd
87 Vauxhall Walk, London SE11 5HJ

This edition published 1994

2 4 6 8 10 9 7 5 3

Text © 1992 Jon Blake
Illustrations © 1992 Axel Scheffler

The right of Jon Blake to be identified as author of this work
has been asserted by him in accordance with the
Copyright, Designs and Patents Act 1988.

Printed in Hong Kong

British Library Cataloguing in Publication Data
A catalogue record for this book is
available from the British Library.

ISBN 0-7445-3158-6

You're a Hero, Daley B!

Written by

Jon Blake

Illustrated by

Axel Scheffler

WALKER BOOKS
AND SUBSIDIARIES
LONDON • BOSTON • SYDNEY

Daley B didn't
know what
he was.

"Am I a monkey?" he said.
"Am I a koala?"
"Am I a porcupine?"

Daley B didn't know where to live.

"Should I live
in a cave?"
he said.

"Should I live in a nest?"

"Should I live in a web?"

Daley B didn't know what to eat.

"Should I
eat fish?"
he said.

"Should I eat potatoes?"

"Should I eat worms?"

Daley B didn't know why his feet were so big.

"Are they for water-skiing?" he said.

"Are they for the mice to sit on?"

"Are they to keep the rain off?"

Daley B saw the birds in the tree, and
decided he would live in a tree.

Daley B saw the squirrels eating acorns,
and decided he would eat acorns.

But he still didn't know why his feet were so big.

One day, there was great panic in the
woodland. All the rabbits gathered
beneath Daley B's tree.
"You must come down at
once, Daley B!" they cried.
"Jazzy D is coming!"
"Who is Jazzy D?" asked Daley B.
The rabbits were too excited to answer.
They scattered across the grass and
vanished into their burrows.

Daley B stayed in his tree, and nibbled another
acorn, and wondered about his big feet.

Jazzy D crept out of the bushes.
Her teeth were as sharp as broken glass, and
her eyes were as quick as fleas.

Jazzy D sneaked around the burrows, but
there was not a rabbit to be seen.

Jazzy D looked up.
Daley B waved.

Jazzy D began to climb the tree.
The other rabbits poked out their
noses, and trembled.

"Hello," said Daley B to Jazzy D.

"Are you a badger?"

"Are you an elephant?"

"Are you a duck-billed platypus?"

Jazzy D crept closer. "No, my friend," she whispered. "I am a weasel."

"Do you live in a pond?" asked Daley B.

"Do you live in a dam?"   "Do you live in a kennel?"

Jazzy D crept closer still.
"No, my friend," she hissed,
"I live in the darkest corner of the wood."

"Do you eat cabbages?" asked Daley B.

"Do you eat insects?"

"Do you eat fruit?"

Jazzy D crept right up to Daley B.
"No, my friend," she rasped, "I eat rabbits!
Rabbits like *you*!"

Daley B's face fell.
"Am I ... a rabbit?" he stammered.

Jazzy D. nodded . . . and licked her lips . . .

and *leapt!*

Daley B didn't have to think. Quick as a flash, he turned his back, and kicked out with his massive feet. Jazzy D sailed through the air, far far away, back where she came from.

The other rabbits jumped and cheered
and hugged each other.
"You're a hero, Daley B!" they cried.

"That's funny," said Daley B.
"I thought I was
a rabbit."

MORE WALKER PAPERBACKS
For You to Enjoy

IMPO

by Jon Blake / Arthur Robins

The uplifting tale of a clapped-out school bus who, to the children's delight,
gets a second life as a hot rod!

0-7445-3144-6   £3.99

SAM WHO WAS SWALLOWED BY A SHARK

by Phyllis Root / Axel Scheffler

Sam, the river rat, dreams of going to sea; it is his heart's desire.
Day and night, whatever he's doing, his thoughts turn seawards. So,
when he sees a chance to build his own boat, he is determined to take it,
no matter what anyone else may say…

"Sparkling pictures." *Naomi Lewis, The Evening Standard*

0-7445-4317-7   £4.50

LITTLE RABBIT FOO FOO

by Michael Rosen / Arthur Robins

A new version of a popular playground rhyme.

"Simple and hilarious… I laugh every time I think about it."
Susan Hill, The Sunday Times

0-7445-2065-7   £4.99

Walker Paperbacks are available from most booksellers, or by post from B.B.C.S., P.O. Box 941, Hull, North Humberside HU1 3YQ

24 hour telephone credit card line 01482 224626

To order, send: Title, author, ISBN number and price for each book ordered, your full name and address,
cheque or postal order payable to BBCS for the total amount and allow the following for postage and packing:
UK and BFPO: £1.00 for the first book, and 50p for each additional book to a maximum of £3.50.
Overseas and Eire: £2.00 for the first book, £1.00 for the second and 50p for each additional book.

Prices and availability are subject to change without notice.